Nativity

Translated
from the French
by Cole Swensen

Nativity by Jean Frémon drawings by Louise Bourgeois

Les Fugitives editions

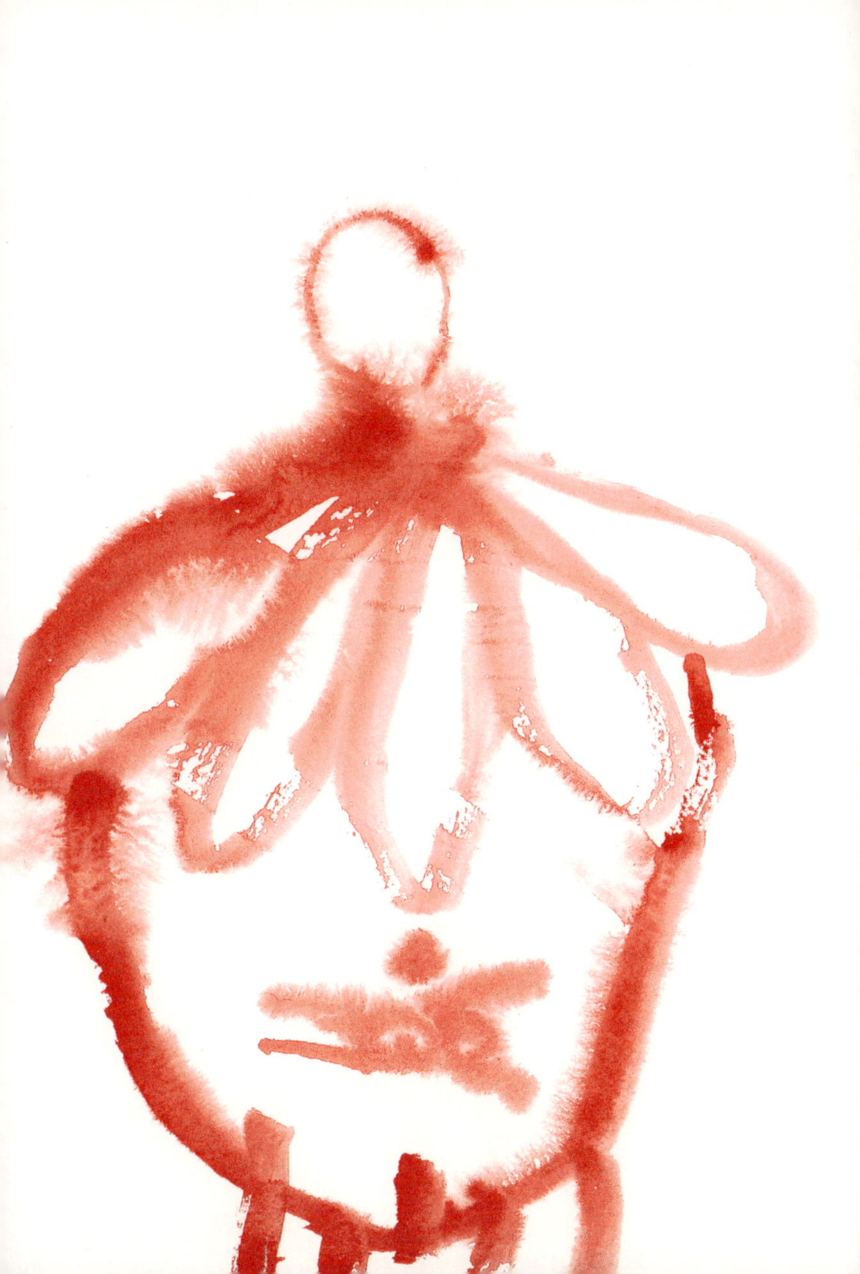

The painter pondered. He bustled about in silence, cleaning his brushes in the clear water, lining up his mortars, smallest to largest, and filing sketches, plans and studies in a leather folder. It kept his hands busy, offered a distraction. He mulled over his task.

A large Nativity on a single panel, the canon had said; narrative altarpieces are no longer in fashion. You'll need to come and measure the palace chapel. Or perhaps an *Adoration*, with shepherds and wise men, if you'd rather, added the canon, but for the same price. Your fee will not be based on the number of horses or camels, but on the way in which you make the incarnation of divinity visible.

No visual tricks, the canon continued; he was an erudite man who spoke in quotations and phrases borrowed from the ancients. The only thing that matters to us is that your painting serve to teach the true faith, nothing else. The doctors write treatises, translate the scriptures, interpret the mysteries; their words are often obscure or ambiguous, and most people don't even know how to read, so it's up to us to decipher them. Your paintings, yours and your guild's, are not just there to decorate the church – they're the only books that the illiterate, those children, can understand. Their faith is so pure. They listen to us, but they also fear us; your images speak to them more clearly than our sermons. You have a huge responsibility, as huge as the power of images on the imagination. We depend on the imagination of painting to prove reality.

This scene occurred around 1360 in Bohemia, where Charles of Luxembourg was on the throne; and in Alsace, in Flanders, in Siena, in Burgundy. Petrarch, inconsolable after the loss of Laura, carried off by the plague, was in the library of St Mark's in Venice. France was caught up in the Jacquerie. In exchange for the écus that got him out of Calais, King Jean, known as the Good, handed his children over to the Visconti. Bayezid, known as the Thunderbolt, was in Adrianopolis, in Thrace, on the Danube and on the Euphrates. Muhammad VI was in Granada. Behind the ramparts of Avignon, Innocent VI preached the need for a crusade against the Bosnian Cathars. Guillaume de Machaut, the canon of Reims cathedral, composed the *Confort d'ami*. In Florence, Brother

Jacopo Talenti finished the campanile. In Milan cathedral, Boccaccio welcomed Leontius Pilatus, the translator of Aristotle. Timur reigned in Samarkand. John VI Kantakouzenos abandoned Byzantium to Palaeologos and retired to Mount Athos, where the Quietists searched for the uncreated light through contemplation of their navels. Everywhere, in Bohemia, in Alsace, in Flanders, in Tuscany, in Burgundy, the same painter asked himself the same question.

It was a time when people readily believed in the unreal, while reality was acknowledged only if reinforced by extensive proofs and guarantees. It was a time when Don Quixote's ancestors rode freely through novels. All that didn't actually exist enjoyed a kind of unlimited capacity for existence, while what actually existed saw its reality ferociously embattled and doubted.

Incarnated divinity – easy for you to say, thought the painter. It is always easy for those who manipulate words; no matter what they say, they will always find a way to claim that they didn't say it or that it was just a figure of speech… for the speaker, writer, preacher or rhetorician, to say that something is a figure of speech is to say: I said this to mean that; there's the letter and then there's the spirit. As a painter, I have to choose to show or not to show. My images cannot say anything other than what they are. What you see is what you see. I have to give body to letter and spirit both. And, sure, I can use symbols – the red carnation, the goldfinch, etc. – but only according to a restrictive code that I must obey.

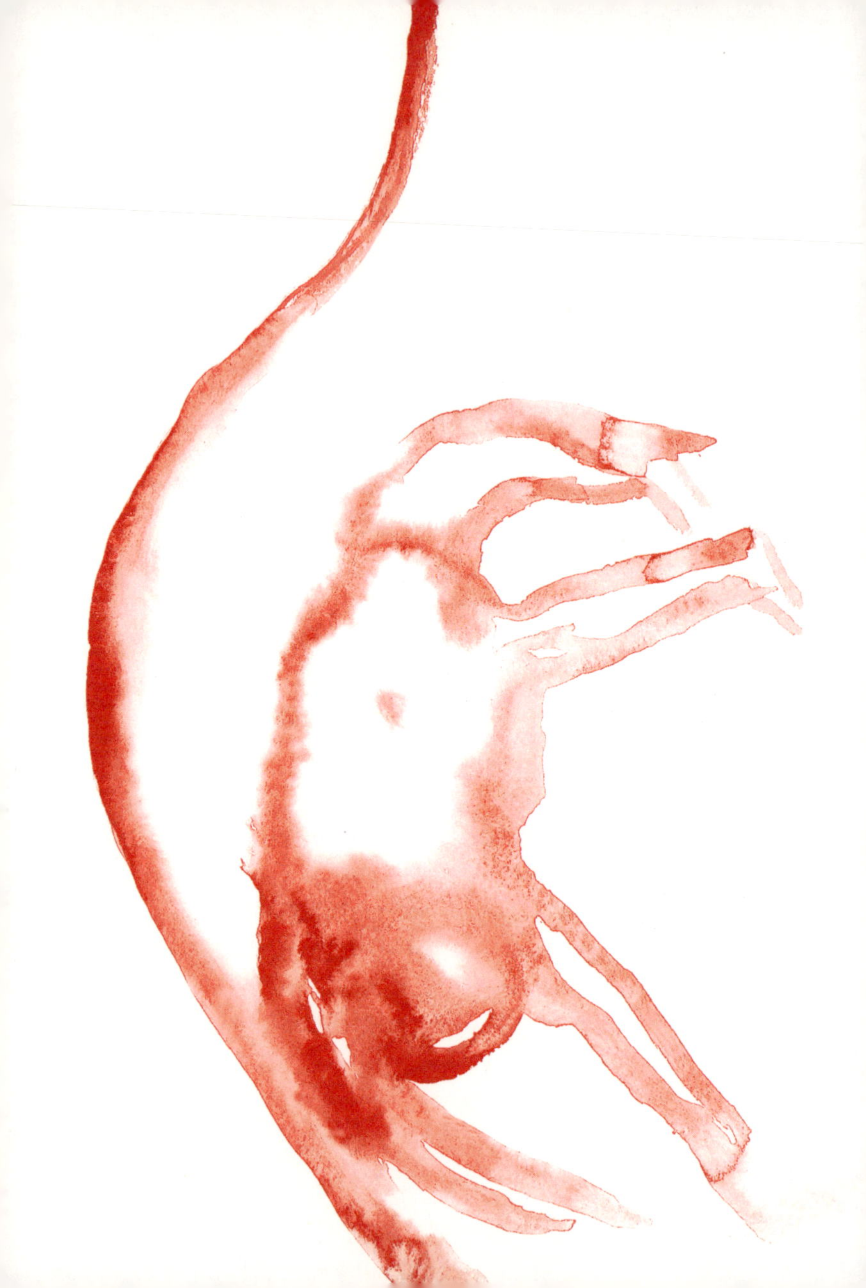

But in the long run, it simply comes down to painting a baby. The ass, the ox, the shepherds, the wise men, they're all no problem. The trick is the baby. The mystery is not that he's God – no one disputes that – it's that this god is a man. That's what I have to show; that's what the canon expects of me. And since the Word was made flesh in order to correct those who search for God in mere appearances, I have to paint this newly formed flesh in all of its attributes.

Complete in all his parts, the canon had said; remember Augustine's words, *complete in all his parts*... He elaborated: the joy of the incarnation. Just as a bird sings its joy at being in the world, our child must swell with joy. And don't think that it will be enough to simply repeat the same old story. You must search within yourself. With the eyes of the soul. The light within you; that's where you must look. In beauty! In sentiment! Not too much sentiment! In mystery! In simplicity! In audacity! In fervour! Be inspired, breathe in the pure air; each morning is a new world. Pray to receive inspiration. God isn't stingy with his guiding lights.

I'm going to show him smiling, said the painter to himself, that'll be new! Aristotle said that no newborn smiles before forty-one days, which is to say, not before mother and child are beyond the danger of post-partum fever. Pliny claimed that the only child ever known to have smiled at birth was Zoroaster. Jesus is as good as Zoroaster, thought the painter. A smile, yes, that's the way to go; my baby Jesus will be a prodigy;

he'll be born smiling at the world. A precocious smile will only underscore the supernatural origin of the child. He picked up a sketchbook and quickly drew a baby's face. With additional short strokes, he rounded out the cheeks, separated the lips, slightly raised the corners of the mouth and lit up the eyes with a point of silvery white. God was delighted to be a man. It was only a sketch, but he visualized the painting that he could make from it. From this smile came light. The heavens were delighted too.

The joy of incarnation – that is the Good News. Fine, he thought, that much is settled. But, as far as I know, the baby Jesus has always been painted with two arms, two legs, a nose and two ears. Complete in all his parts; it seemed that the holy man had wanted to say something else – could he have been hinting that I should also give the baby boy a little penis and two little balls? He couldn't quite put it into words, but he did say complete in all his parts – work it out from there, you image-maker.

Christ and sex – right off, the two words seem mutually exclusive. The word *sin* separates them and keeps them forever at a distance. The former is exempt from it, and the latter is immersed in it. And for precisely that reason, bringing them together in an image would be the strongest and surest way to create surprise and strike the senses.

Byzantine icons showed no sign of the flesh except for the face and hands and perhaps a naked foot behind a veil. It was considered that the face displayed the divine nature, and only the foot proclaimed the human. The Sienese usually showed the baby Jesus dressed in the long tunic and cloak of a philosopher. Later, he was depicted wearing children's clothes that the people of Tuscany sometimes hemmed up to the knee. Isn't it clear where they're heading? asked the painter. But Nativities always show a baby enveloped in yards of linen. Luke had written: Mary wrapped him in swaddling clothes and laid him in a manger. Neither Matthew, Mark, nor John mentioned it, but Luke did. The canon has asked more of me. He wants me to show what is usually hidden.

Traditionally, sculptors from the Rhine carved their crucifixes from wood, enveloping the hips of the tortured man in a cloth soaked in plaster. The painter remembered one such sculptor, whom he had met in his master's studio, who had, with great devotion, sculpted perfectly proportioned genitalia before masking them with the plaster-soaked cloth. It's not nothing that we're hiding from sight, he thought. He had emphasized the protuberance by positioning the knot of the loincloth exactly at the right place to suggest that the penis might be erect behind its veil. They had talked about it for hours at the tavern. Claus was a pious man who had spent years reading the scriptures. He had worked in Dijon for Philip the Bold, the Duke of Burgundy. He had had the audacity to go beyond Gothic rigidity and had become famous for a group of prophets that formed the base of a large crucifix. The way that he had created the curves and folds with his chisel was wonderful to see; the turban on Daniel's head remained a venerated example, as did the cloth around Jesus's waist. He said that the genitals, which he had carved out of pear wood, the hardest he could find, demonstrated the human nature of Christ. Out of modesty, he had hidden it under the loincloth, but in such a way that it was still perceptible. He went so far as to suggest that the erection, the supposed cause of the bulge of knotted cloth, should be understood as a symbol of the resurrection of the flesh. In addition, the heavenward angle of the member and its veil, he claimed, gave his composition the dramatic force needed to convince even the most sceptical.

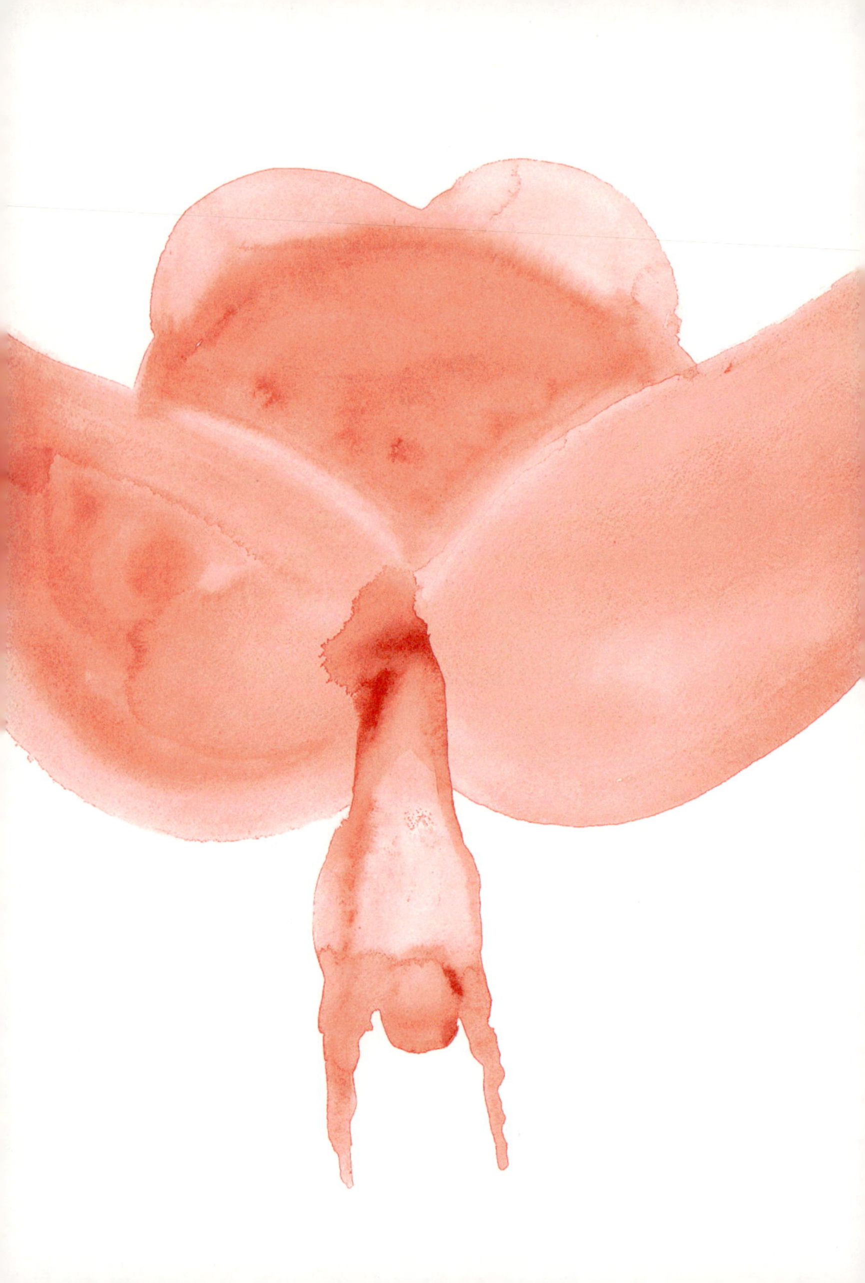

The painter dreamed of translating this idea into paint if the canon ever commissioned a Crucifixion. A three-quarter view of the cross, rather than the usual frontal perspective, would allow the knotted cloth in front of the angled hips to stand out against the cloudy sky. A strong wind would blow a bit of the cloth up into the air, implying the reaching of the flesh towards its resurrection at the moment of death. But the next day, he vigorously rejected the idea as too exaggerated and opted instead for a diaphanous veil through which the genitalia would be visible, as it had been through the waters of the River Jordan in the *Baptism of Christ* that his master had painted in his studio in the via del Cocomero. A veil as light as water, he thought, and under that veil, the proof that the canon required.

But for the moment, it was a Nativity that he had to deliver.

The painter was ambitious; he dreamed of having a huge studio with a flock of young assistants. He'd be jealous of their youth, of course, but he would conscientiously mentor the most gifted among them, and his name would become known far beyond the province. The first step was to dazzle and awe the canon. Feeling that he would have to risk indecency, the painter thought of his friend Taddeo's *Madonna and Child*, in which the hand of the Virgin had drifted towards the top of the naked thigh of the child who stood on his mother's knee. The combination of the Virgin's gesture and her gaze solidly meeting that of the viewer made it perfectly clear: Look at what I'm showing

you; understand what I'm telling you
– the proof of the incarnation is here; the
completeness that Augustine demanded
is at the tips of my fingers. Complete in
all his parts, he had said.

And in another Madonna and Child,
the Virgin looks at the child, who is taking
her breast in both of his hands to bring it
to his mouth, while the child himself
looks insistently at the viewer, seeming
to say: See, I am human; I nurse from
my mother's breast. I need terrestrial
nourishment, just like you. And is that not
a new miracle? He suckles in profile but
looks at you straight on. I've never seen
a baby at his mother's breast who could
do that. But this one? A miracle, I say.

Go further? Unveil everything? Eliminate
the swaddling clothes? A naked infant

in a stable at Christmas – that's not reasonable. Even in Palestine, it must be cold in December. They were poor people, leaving in a hurry for Bethlehem in order to obey the edict for the census; they took nothing with them. But loving parents, even those who had nothing, would never leave their baby naked on a bed of straw. Would a good mother keep her warm cloak on instead of using it to cover her baby? One more reason, he thought. If it's not natural for the child to be naked, they'll understand why I've undressed him. Mary is not a bad mother. And naked, this child is not cold. Does he look cold? He's radiant. We're in Palestine, but we're not in Palestine. It's winter, but it's not winter. We're in the time and place of the image and of what it has to say to the world, thought the painter.

His decision made, he did what no one before him had done. Pliny said that Polygnotus was the first to paint a woman with her body visible beneath a transparent veil. His paintings have disappeared, but his name remains. A new Pliny will write my name; I will be the first to dare to show the infant naked, to go beyond Luke's writings, to defy all reason. This innovation must occupy the centre of a large composition, and everything else must be geometrically organized around the little body displaying its attributes.

Nakedness is its own light, thought the painter.

Fired up by his new resolution, the painter grabbed his sketchbook and began to draw the contours of an overhanging rock under which he would place the Virgin. Joseph would be a little off to the side, leaning on the rock. This crèche would be more of a grotto than a stable. Then he would place the baby in the bottom of a manger, on a small pile of straw borrowed from the animals' stalls. Just behind the manger, in the shadows of the night, two enormous heads, one of an ass and one of an ox – he roughly sketched them in – gazed with amazement at the miracle before their eyes. They breathed in unison... he dreamed his painting... their unified breathing warmed the little naked body and formed a halo around him, tinting the supernatural light emanating from the child, who smiled with well-being. The Good News was within him. No candle, no lantern; it's night, it's a stable; all the light comes from Him; it illumi-nates the face of the Virgin leaning over

the improvised cradle, as well as those of
the angels. He watches them descend,
three, four, then five, robed in white, five
tiny, unreal faces framed in long blonde
curls. They had rushed to the scene;
the last one still had his wings spread
open. They knelt before the manger,
hands clasped or held up in a sign of
astonishment. And so nine pairs of eyes,
from all sides of the painting, converged
on a single point: there were Joseph's
– he was standing in the background
shadows, his hand over his heart; there
were Mary's, the good mother – a white
veil surrounded her porcelain face with
its two almond eyes and her eyebrows
raised, so that the oval of her face alone
received the light that rose up toward
her; there were the large, affectionate
eyes of the ox, open wide; those of the
ass, a bit narrower and soft as a doe's,

with long curving eyelashes; and there were the small round eyes of the band of angels, simple black points, but overflowing with devotion and reverence – all these gazes converged at the bottom of the canvas on the body of the infant and his insolently erect little penis.

That's the miracle, they all seemed to silently say: God is a man, and he's smiling at the world.

God is made flesh, said the luminous angel who could be seen in the sky revealed by a hole in the roof of the dilapidated stable. The angel was talking to several shepherds on a hillside watching over their flocks. They were gathered around a wood fire, which was the custom twice a year, once for the shortest night and once for the longest.

The angel urged them to go as quickly as they could to confirm for themselves his news: a king had been born in whom divinity and humanity were united, as well as majesty and weakness, the sublime and the base, and the eternal, the ancient and the new.

There it was, for the canon, a simple Nativity in the calm of the night. I could do a good-sized painting based on this sketch in twenty days at the outside, thought the painter, his head full of the singing of the angels that he had gathered together in his sketchbook. Then he turned the page and, carried away by enthusiasm, quickly put down even more pencil lines, which amounted to an even more complex composition. It will be an *Adoration of the Magi* like no one has ever seen before, he thought.

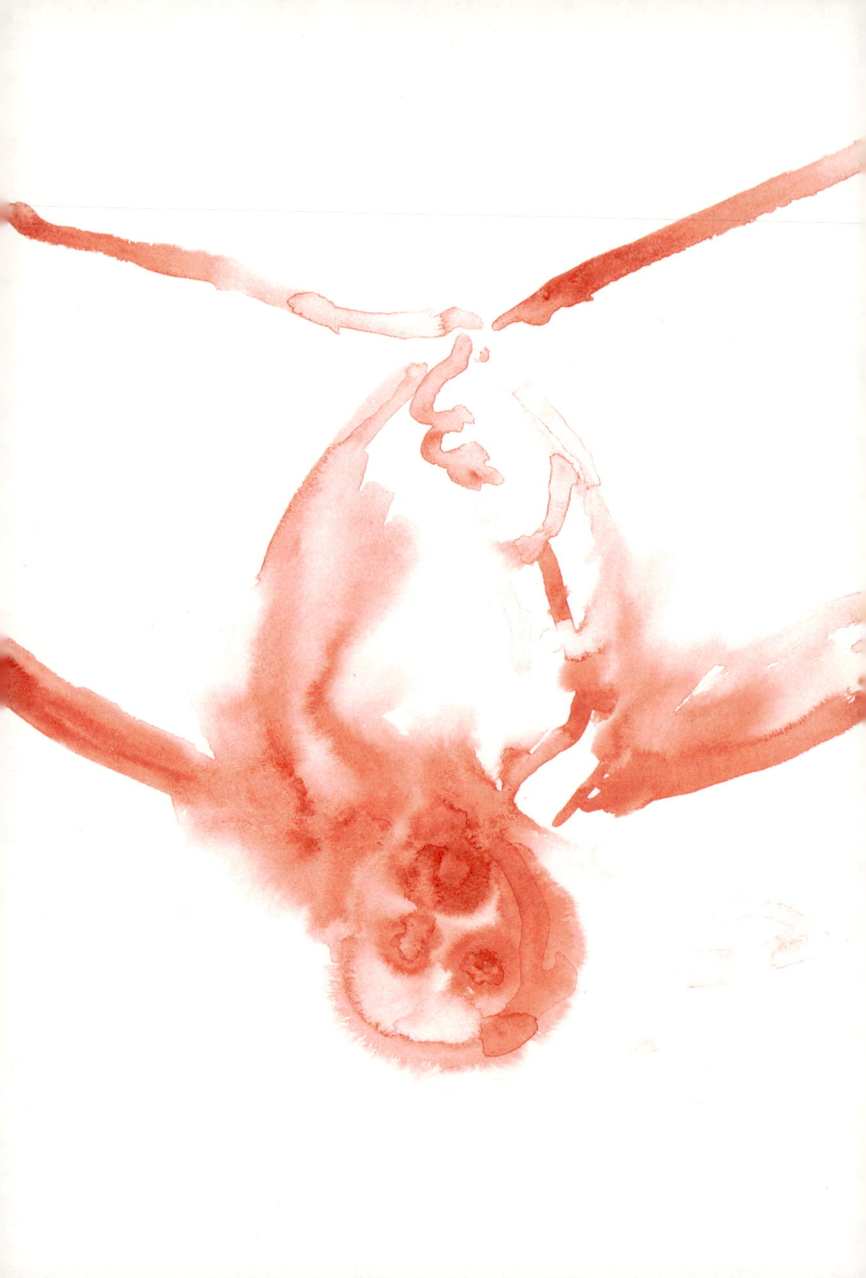

From the left and from the right, great crowds unfurled; it was an immense cortège coming from the great distance of the top of the painting, snaking down the flank of a mountain. Nobles on horseback, vassals on foot with their lances and helmets, as if they were setting off on a crusade. They had come a long way; from time to time, one left the file to hunt a deer to feed the people. The kings and their retinues were grouped tightly together in the foreground. Their names in Latin were Appellius, Amerius and Damascus; in Hebrew, Galgalat, Malgalat and Sarachin; in Greek, Gaspar, Balthazar and Melchior. The first was the King of Arabia, the second, the King of India, and the third, the King of Persia. Those perched on the Mountain of Victory who keep an eye out for omens had seen a star and had ordered them to follow it. A king had been born, and they must pay him homage; the star would show them the way. They brought offerings of gold, frankincense and myrrh – gold as a sign of love and to alleviate the poverty of the parents, frankincense as a sign of prayer and to dissipate the strong odours of the stable, and myrrh to cover the child's naked body and to repel the vermin that infect all flesh.

A palpable shiver, a ripple, ran through the painted crowd. Some of them, wearing red hats, tried to catch the viewers' eyes, as if to invite them to join in the action they were watching, while others seemed to relay this look, guiding viewers towards the centre of the composition, where the oldest of the kings, a bald man with a grey beard, was kneeling and bowing deeply before the evident majesty of the child. Next to him on the ground, he had placed his crown and his coffer. Bareheaded, as a sign of humility, he seemed about to kiss the tiny foot he held in the hollow of his hand. In a gesture that seemed perfectly natural, the mother extended the other leg, which she held by the thigh. The child himself, all smiles, participated in the demonstration by raising the transparent veil that fell from his shoulders. And whoever follows the doubting gaze of the old king must admit that it falls directly between the baby's legs and nowhere else. There is the proof of his humanity. The mother's gaze, as well as the child's, is also aimed at this incontrovertible, clinical proof and seems to encourage others to look too. The King of Arabia knew that a messiah had been born; the prophets had announced it, and the omens had confirmed it, which is why he had made the journey following the star. The King of India and the King of Persia, witnesses to the same omens from even greater distances, had joined him. What the kings had come to verify and what they announced to all and that all repeated was not so much that a god had been born, but that he was a man, the divine pecker between his chubby thighs proved it. A miracle, he said; the Son of Man is a man.

It was the eighth day; the child was taken to the temple and his flesh was cut with a stone knife. 'You back there, you unrighteous Sedecians, and you, Valencians, Alexandrians, Manichaeans, Basilidians, Apelites, preachers of lies, utterly reject your old beliefs. This body is not imaginary, nor celestial, nor spiritual – a fantasy body doesn't bleed. Who can claim that this has been faked, who can deny that this most fragile member has been cut and has suffered and bled. Where and when have you, you doubting heretics, ever seen an illusion that bleeds,' demanded the King of Arabia. In the background, the horses of the three kings, one black, one white and one brown, exchanged knowing looks, as if they had known all along what their masters had just discovered.

The painter closed his sketchbook; all he had to do now was to get down to work. I have no doubt that you'll know just what to do, the canon had said. And for a long time after him, it was inconceivable to depict the infant Jesus other than with his attributes fully visible and often highlighted by a gesture or the converging lines of perspective. Until another canon, a hundred other canons (the faith having sunk into idiocy), hired a hundred other painters called clothiers to adorn the canvases of the old masters with veils, leaves, bunches of fruit or simply underclothes, in order to mask that which offends stupidity. They were men who didn't like humanity, and the idea that one was a god repulsed them. They preferred to replace an ancient tale told in all sincerity with a devious fabrication that, they believed, would ensure their everlasting power over a weak-minded citizenry.

The Counter-Reformation apparently did not understand what the Pre-Renaissance had astutely suggested by the image. Francisco Pacheco, in his *Art of Painting*, was distressed to see painters representing Jesus naked in the arms of his mother, who was decently, even quite richly, dressed. He said that painters who did this were claiming that a child is more beautiful naked than dressed or even that the nudity was supposed to emphasize the poverty of the Lord. He did not know that the power of an image is proportional to its capacity for mystery.

And it wasn't so long ago – with the arrival of photography – that there occurred an iconoclastic reaction against such prudishness. Images that were known for hiding this mark of immo-desty were, before being reproduced in books, retouched with the details that had, without a word, proclaimed that the god that man sought throughout the night was none other than himself.

It is said that He made man in His image. Or was it, in fact, the other way around? And, in fact, it was a painter, a maker of images, who managed to achieve what all the Evangelists could only suggest: to declare divine, in the form of a child, this species that hates itself so much as to impose on itself such martyrdom, which, like all species, dies and is reborn.

And it requires the image, the generative instrument, suddenly unveiled, of a baby in the middle of winter or a dying man, tortured and stretched out under a shroud, on a Friday afternoon in spring (does the mandrake also grow at the foot of the cross?) to make it clear that the promised resurrection is none other than that of the species that regenerates itself throughout eternity.

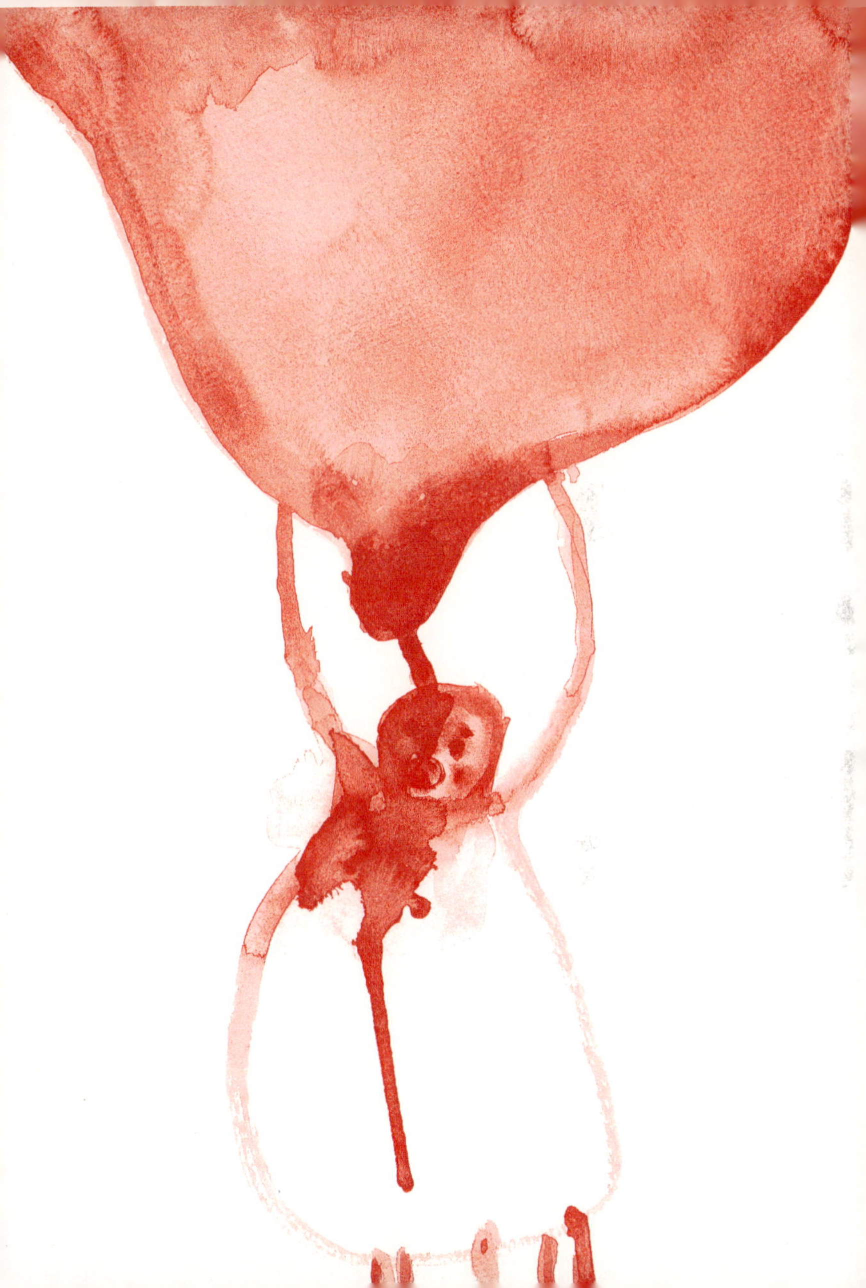

Beginning in the early 1980s, when I was in New York I would visit Louise Bourgeois either at her home or at her Brooklyn studio. In Brooklyn, she would show me her latest sculptures, while at her house in Manhattan (and in her last years, she no longer went out to Brooklyn, so it was always in Chelsea) she would show me her recent drawings and prints. One day in 2007, I discovered an entirely new series of drawings. They were silhouettes of women with embryos in their wombs, drawn with a brush full of water and red gouache. These drawings were, for me, the most poignant of her long career. Each time I visited, Louise would ask me about what I was writing. It was a kind of ritual that always made me a little uneasy, and I never knew quite how to respond. But Louise liked making her visitors a little uneasy.

But that particular day, it was very simple – I had just written a short piece that took almost all of its argumentation from Leo Steinberg's seminal book *The Sexuality of Christ in Renaissance Art and in Modern Oblivion*. I can sum it up easily, I said: it's the story of the first painter who had the idea of representing the baby Jesus completely naked rather than in swaddling clothes. The parallels between the story and her drawings of pregnancy and birth struck us both. Louise asked me for the text, which I sent to her. When I next came to visit her, five drawings were awaiting me to illustrate the book.

The 2009 French edition was published by Fata Morgana on the 25th of December, the birthday not only of Jesus, but also of Louise Bourgeois. Several weeks later, Louise signed the fifteen books that made up the limited edition.

Even though it's very short, the text doesn't borrow only from Leo Steinberg; throughout, it contains words and ideas from Clément Rosset, Frank Stella, Claus Sluter, Bartolo di Fredi, Benozzo Gozzoli, Geertgen tot Sint Jans, Rogier van der Weyden, Domenico Ghirlandaio, Joan Miró, Vincent van Gogh, St Augustine, Antonio Lollio, Franciscus Cardulus, Edward Gibbon and Emmanuel Hocquard.

Jean Frémon

This first English edition
published in Great Britain in November 2020
by Les Fugitives, reprinted in 2023
91 Cholmley Gardens, Fortune Green Road, London NW6 1UN
www.lesfugitives.com

Originally published by Éditions Fata Morgana in 2009, as
Naissance, and in *Rue du regard* © P.O.L. Éditeur, 2012
English language translation © Cole Swensen 2020

Cover and text design by David Massabuau (Fata Morgana)

Original gouache drawings on paper by Louise Bourgeois
© The Easton Foundation / VAGA at ARS,
NY and DACS, London 2020

The good mother, 2007, 19,8 x 22,8 cm
Pregnant woman, 2008, 37,1 x 27,9 cm
The birth, 2007, 59,6 x 45,7 cm
The birth, 2007, 60 x 45,7 cm
The bad mother, 1998, 37,1 x 27,9 cm

Photographs by Christopher Burke.

A CIP catalogue record for this book
is available from the British Library.
The rights of Jean Frémon and Cole Swensen
to be identified respectively as author and translator
of this work have been identified in accordance with
Section 77 of the Copyright, Designs and Patents Act 1988.

Printed in England by CMP, Poole, Dorset